序に

大海原の水平線に
いま昇るがごとく
太陽を背に舞う
平将門揚羽之君
宇宙の音色と共に
始まる現代の神話

企画・原案／玉塚充

Introduction

As if he is just about to rise
From the horizon of the open sea,
Taira no Masakado Ageha no Kimi
Dances with the sun—
A contemporary Myth
Opening with the Sound of Space

Conceived and Directed by Mitsuru Tamatsuka

七千億年先の地球にも まだヒトはいた。
地球は もはや何もない空間だった。
だからヒトは かつての人類を想像しながら くらしていた。
それをヒトは **オモカゲ**と呼んでいた。

何もない地球はオモカゲであふれていた。
そこには色がなく 温もりもなかった。

それでもヒトは平気だった。
かつての地球を想像しながら そのオモカゲといっしょにヒトは生きていた。

そんな地球に トウキョウと呼ばれる街を想像しながら生きる 小さなヒトがいた。

オモカゲのトウキョウを生きる 一人の少年がいた。

Seven hundred billion years in the future, on Earth humans still live.
Earth is now just an empty space.
So the humans live imagining the men of the past.
And the humans call these **Shadows**.

The empty Earth is filled with Shadows.
There are no colors and no warmth.

But still, humans live on.
Humans imagine the past Earth and live alongside these Shadows.

There on Earth is a small human living on while imagining a city called Tokyo.

There is a boy living in the Shadow of Tokyo.

春、
アゲハチョウは、そよそよと舞っていた。今か今かと待っていた。
あの男が射止めるものが、なんなのかを見逃すまいと。

腕は確かだ。あの男が流鏑馬の稽古をしている時、
百発百中で的を射るのを盗み見ていたのは、このアゲハチョウたちだった。

実は、かの宇多天皇の御代、菅原道真公が流鏑馬の稽古に励むのを見守ったのもこのアゲハチョウたちだった。
それどころか、三島由紀夫が金閣寺に参詣した際、小説のアイディアを着想し、手帳に書き出しをメモするのも盗み見たし、
ジョン・レノンが暗殺されたのをニューヨークの高級住宅の玄関アーチの模様に化けて目撃したのも、このアゲハチョウたちだった！

ローマ皇帝ジュリアス・シーザーがブルータスに…木からリンゴが落ちるのをニュートンが見て…アポロが月面に到着したのを…

嗚呼、挙げればキリがない！
このアゲハチョウたちはあらゆる出来事を盗み見てきたのだ！

彼らは、その度に思ったものだ。
「誰もが何かを探している。が、探し求めているものをはっきりと見つけ出し、その的の中心を的確に射抜く者は、ほとんどいない。
しかし、その射抜いた先に、幸せがあるかといえば、それは、どうだろうか…。」

春、
アゲハチョウたちは、舞っていた。男が矢を射るのを、待っていた。
あの男には、誰かのオモカゲがある。
あの男の射止めるものがなんなのか、アゲハチョウたちは意識を集中させた。

In the spring breeze,
The swallowtail butterflies softly fluttered by. Waiting for the moment to arrive.
Not to miss what that man will bring down with his arrow.

His aim was certain. These swallowtails were the ones secretly watching him strike home, ten out of ten, during his *yabusame*[1] training.

As a matter of fact, these swallowtails were the ones that watched Michizane Sugawara train for *yabusame* during the reign of Emperor Uda.
Not only that, but these swallowtails secretly watched Mishima visit Kinkakuji, and inspired, jot down on his notebook the idea for his novel.
And they were also the ones who witnessed John Lennon's assassination, disguised as the pattern of an archway in Upper West Side New York!

When the Roman emperor Julius Caesar was, by Brutus ... when the apple dropped from the tree, and Newton ...
when the Apollo landed on the surface of the moon ...

Oh, how the list goes on!
These swallowtails have secretly witnessed countless incidents!

And at each moment, they thought,
"Everyone is seeking for something. But so few people actually discover what they are searching for and drive through its heart. But then again, whether nailing the heart of the matter leads to happiness, well, that's something else..."

In the Spring breeze,
The swallowtail butterflies fluttered.
Waiting for the man to shoot the arrow.
There is a Shadow of someone in that man.

The swallowtails concentrated their senses, and they watched for what that man was going to shoot.

(1) A game of hitting the mark with a whistling arrow while galloping on horseback

少年は、オモカゲのトウキョウの入り口へたどり着く。
そこには巨大な地図がある。

それは、人体解剖図のような地図だ。

人間の頭の部分が大きなお堀になっていて、その真ん中にエド城がある。
天守、本丸、二の丸、三の丸は脳味噌のようで、全体はまるでドクロだ。

そのドクロから体の方へ、道路や列車の路線が血管のように伸びている。
ヤマノテ線、チュウオウ線、マルノウチ線、カンジョウ線…。

小さな毛細血管のような小道が隅々まで張り巡らされ、体の各部位へとたどり着く。

ロッポン木は右手の薬指、アキハ原は左の掌、シブ谷はヘソ、カミナリ門は喉仏、カブキ座は肺、
カスミガ関は突き出たお腹、ニホン橋は太もも、ユウラク町は十二指腸、ギン座は腹筋の割れ目…。

オモカゲのトウキョウは、巨大な男のようだ。

少年は、その人体模型図のような地図を見つめながら、行き先を定める。
急所を狙うスナイパーのような目つきで。
今日の目的地がどこにあるのかを、決して間違わないように。

The boy reaches the entrance of the Shadow of Tokyo.
Standing there is a huge map.

The map is like an anatomical chart.

The head of the man is a big moat, and the *Edo* Castle is in its center.
The tower, donjon, outer citadel and the outermost regions of the castle are like the brain tissue, and in its entirety it is like a *skull*.

Roads and railways extend from the *skull* to the body like blood vessels.
The *Yamanote* line, *Chuo* line, *Marunouchi* line, *Inner Circular* Route …

Paths like small capillaries stretch into every corner, reaching each region of the body.
Roppongi is the ring finger of the right hand, *Akihabara* is the left palm, *Shibuya* is the navel, *Kaminari-mon* is the thyroid cartilage,
Kabuki-za is the lungs, *Kasumigaseki* is the protruding potbelly, *Nihonbashi* is the thighs, *Yurakucho* is the duodenum, *Ginza* is the groove
between the abdominal muscles …

The Shadow of Tokyo is like a huge man.

The boy stares straight into this anatomical chart-like map and ponders where to go.
Like a sniper, taking his aim at a fatal spot. So as not to be mistaken where his destination today shall be.

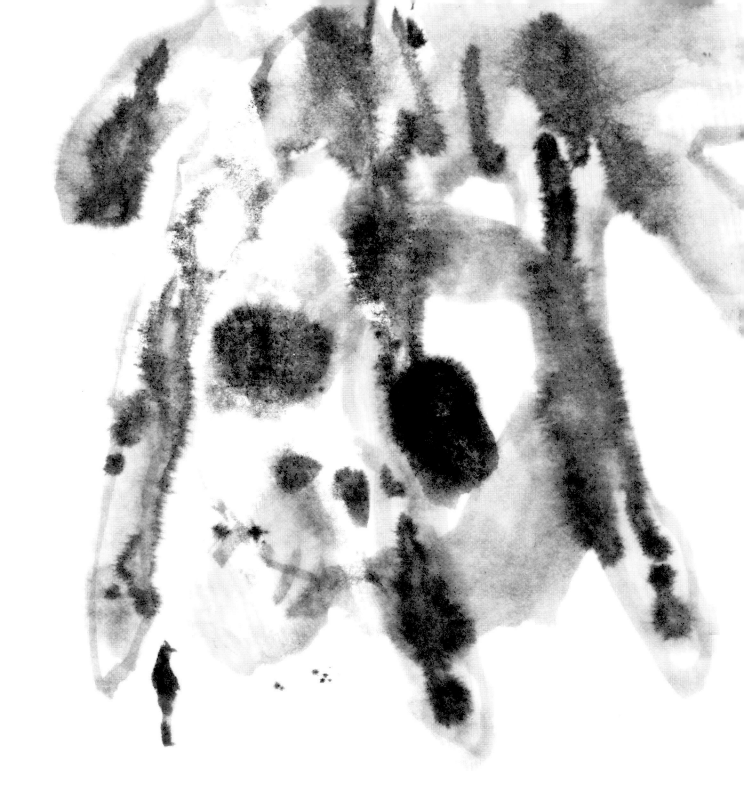

男は、力の限りに矢を放った！
ビューンッ！
彼の腕は引きちぎられんばかりだ。
その一矢は、人民たちの希望だ。
圧政からの解放、伝染病による滅びと喪失からの回復。

ビュワアアアアアー!! グサアアアアアー!! ウワアアアアアー!!
その矢は、獲物を射抜いた！

シーン…。

男は身動き一つしない。
どれだけの時間が流れただろうか。

アゲハチョウはいつの間にか、男のそばを舞っていた。そよそよと。
そして、耳もとでささやいた。
「あなたは、この世界を守りたい？」
「…。」
「でもそれはもう失敗したかもしれない。」
「…。」
「あなたは矢を放った。その矢が射抜いたもの、それを確認した？」
「…。」
男の全身から、汗が吹き出した。
「あなたは、それを見に行かなくてはならない。
この世界で、あなたが射抜いたものがなんなのか、
それを自分の目で確かめなくてはならない。」

男の目は血走っていた。振り向こうか迷った。
迷いは隙をうんだ。そして身をかわそうとした、その刹那！
グワアアアアアー!!
世界は真っ暗闇となった！

「…。」男は、息絶えた。

アゲハチョウたちのオモカゲは、もうそこにはいなかった。
平安時代に似つかわしい、だだっ広い平野がそこにはあるだけだ。

少し変わったことといえば、
ただ、BEATLES の "Love Me Do" が
関東平野一帯に響き渡っているということくらいだ。

The man shot the arrow with all his might!
ZOOOOM!
His arms were on the verge of ripping apart.
This arrow carried the hopes of the people.
Liberation from tyranny; restoration from the ruins
and losses brought by the pandemic.

SWOOOOSH!! THWAAAACK!! YEAHHHHHHH!!
The arrow struck its target on the mark!

And it was silent …

The man did not move an inch.
How much time had passed?

Without notice,
the swallowtails were fluttering by the man. Softly.
And they whispered in his ear.
"Do you want to save this world?"
"…"
"But you may have already failed."
"…"
"You shot the arrow. Did you see what you pierced with that arrow?"
"…"
Sweat poured out from all over the man's body.
"You must go see it.
You must go see with your own eyes what you shot in this world."

The man's eyes were bloodshot. The man wavered, whether he should turn
around or not. The hesitation made him drop his guard. And he tried to
dodge it, but at that instant …!
ARGGGGGGGGGG!!
The world became pitch black!
"…" The man breathed his last.

The Shadows of the swallowtails were there no more.
There was only a vast plain, just as suits the Heian Era.

The only odd thing was that, "Love Me Do"
by the BEATLES was ringing across the whole Kanto Plain.

トゥ〜ル〜、ルッルッル。トゥトゥトゥトゥ〜トゥ〜、ルッルッル。
少年は、ハーモニカを吹いている。正確にいえば、ハーモニカの**オモカゲ**だ。

人体解剖型の地図によれば、目的地へはおよそ十八里。歩けない距離じゃない。
少年はそのオモカゲのハーモニカを演奏しながら歩きはじめた。
人類がかつて聞いていたメロディーのオモカゲを奏でながら。

ラ〜ブ、ラ〜ブ、ミー、ドゥー！　ユ〜、ノ〜ウ、アイ、ラブユー！

それに引き寄せられるように、たくさんの動物たちのオモカゲが、少年のうしろからついてくる。
タヌキ、キツネ、ネコ、ブタ、ウサギ、カラス、クマ、ウシ、ウマ…。

少年を先頭にした行列が歩みを進めるごとに、オモカゲのトウキョウには調和がうまれる。

ズンチャン！　ズンチャン！　ズンチャン！

メロディーは続く。オモカゲの太陽が山々に上ったかと思うと、山の端にオモカゲの月が照り、
白黒の星々がオモカゲの大地に降り注ぐ。

行列は進む。オモカゲのトウキョウの先にあるオモカゲの海へと。
トゥ〜ル〜、ルッルッル。トゥトゥトゥトゥ〜トゥ〜、ルッルッル…

TRRRR TRRRR TU-LU-TU. TU-TU-LU TRRRR TRRRR TU-LU-TU.
The boy is playing his harmonica.
To be precise, he is blowing the **Shadow** of a harmonica.

According to the anatomical chart map, it is approximately eighteen miles to his destination. Not a distance he cannot walk.
The boy started walking, playing his harmonica. Playing the Shadow of a melody humans once listened to.

LOVE, LOVE ME DO! YOU KNOW I LOVE YOU!

As if drawn to this melody, the Shadows of many animals follow behind the boy. Raccoons, foxes, cats, pigs, rabbits, crows, bears, cows, horses…

As the boy and his procession pace on forward, colors spread over the Shadow of Tokyo.

BOOM CHINNG! BOOM CHINNG! BOOM CHINNG!

The melody rings on. The Shadow of the sun threads over the mountains,
soon followed by the Shadow of the moon shining across the mountainside, and monochrome stars shower over the Shadow of the ground.

The procession continues. Heading for the Shadow of the sea, lying beyond the Shadow of Tokyo.
TRRRR TRRRR TU-LU-TU. TU-TU-LU TRRRR TRRRR TU-LU-TU…

少年は目的地にたどり着く。そこは海だ。
オモカゲの海…

オモカゲの海のことを想像している時だけが、
彼は彼自身の世界の住人だった。
海のオモカゲを彼は愛した。

何万年も前に海は失われていた。
何色かと問われても、どんな音がそこにあるのか、
誰も答えることができなかった。

全ては白黒だった。

彼は、砂浜に座って、耳を澄ませた。
しかし、無音だ…

少年は、想像するよりほかなかった。
少年は記憶の中にある全ての音を消していった。
全てを消して、浮かび上がってくる音だけが欲しかった。
波の音のオモカゲに集中した。

白黒の海。無音の海。

少年は海に色をつけようとした。
少年は海に音をつけたかった。

彼は動物たちを丁寧に見渡した。

彼らの中にドックドックと流れる色があった。
彼らの中にドックドックと聞こえる音があった。

少年は、動物たちの中に確かに海があるのを感じた。

同時に彼は動物たちと同じように自分の中にも
同じ海があるのを感じた。

白黒の海の向こう側にオモカゲの太陽が昇りはじめた。

ドック、ドック、ドック、ドック、ドック。

少年の中にはもう音楽はなかった。Love me do は鳴らなかった。

少年はポケットに忍ばせていた短剣を取り出した。
正確には短剣のオモカゲだ。

動物たちが見守っている。

モノクロの太陽が燦々と照りつけ、海がうごめきはじめた。

ドック、ドック、ドック、ドック、ドック。

少年は海に色をつけようとした。

彼は、短剣の矛先を動物たちにはっきりと見えるように
高々と掲げた。

白黒の海に、真っ白な太陽光線が照りつける。
うごめく海は、無音だ。

少年は短剣をドックドックと聞こえる方へと、勢いよく刺した。

バタッと倒れた。
少年の中をドックドックと流れる色が世界にあふれた。

海には、いつのまにか、真っ赤な太陽が昇っていた。

動物たちは、倒れた少年を見て、泣いていた。

その涙の流れる音が、波の音へと変化していく。

耳を済ますと、いつの間にか、
真っ赤な太陽光線で輝く海には、音が聞こえていた。

14

The boy arrives to his destination. It is the sea.
A Shadow of the sea …

Only when he is imagining the Shadow of the sea was he alive in his world.
He loved the Shadow of the sea.

The seas were lost tens of thousands of years ago.
Even if asked its color, no one could tell what sounds there were.

Everything was monochrome.

He sat on the seashore, and listened carefully to the sound.
But there was nothing ….

The boy could only imagine.
The boy silenced each and every sound in his memory.
He only wanted the sounds that would emerge after he silenced everything.
He concentrated on the Shadow of the sound of the waves.

The colorless sea. The silent sea.

The boy tried to add colors to the sea.
The boy tried to add sounds to the sea.

He looked around carefully at the animals.

There were colors flowing rhythmically within them.
There were sounds thumping rhythmically within them.

The boy felt that there was indeed a sea inside the animals.

And he could feel the same sea inside himself, as in the animals.

The Shadow of the sun began to rise across the monochrome sea.

Thump, thump, thump, thump, thump.

There was no music inside the boy anymore.
Love Me Do played no more.

The boy took out the dagger he had slipped in his pocket.
To be accurate, the Shadow of a dagger.

The animals were watching over him.

The blazing white sun showered over the sea, and the sea began to move.

Thump, thump, thump, thump, thump.

The boy tried to color the sea.

He raised the blade of his dagger high so all the animals could see it.

The blazing white sunlight shone across the monochrome sea.
The moving sea was silent.

The boy took his dagger and drove it down into
where he could hear the thumping.

He dropped to the ground. The colors thumping through
the boy flooded into the world.

Silently, a scarlet sun had risen above the sea.

The animals, seeing the boy on the ground, wept.

The sound of tears changes into the sound of waves.

If you listen carefully, a sound could be heard coming from the sea,
shimmering in the scarlet sunlight.

男の魂は平安時代の関東平野を捨てて、空へと舞い上がる。

少年の魂はオモカゲのトウキョウを捨てて、宙へと舞い上がる。

地上と天上の間には、巨大な無数の橋が伸びていて、死んだ魂たちはその橋を渡っていく。

巨大ないくつもの橋は交差し、絡み合い、らせん状だ。

そこには時空のねじれがあり、あらゆる魂たちで大混雑している。

さながら魂のスクランブル交差点。

いかなる時代の、いかなる生命の魂もこの交差点を横断する。

その交差点の真ん中で、平安時代を生きた男の魂と、
オモカゲの東京を生きた少年の魂が、偶然すれ違う。
その瞬間、引き寄せられるように、二つの魂が絡み合う。

戯れるアゲハチョウのように。

二つの魂は舞い、そして、対話する。

The man's soul abandoned the Kanto Plain and soared into the sky.

The boy's soul abandons the Shadow of Tokyo and soars into the air.

Countless gigantic bridges stretched from the ground to the heavens,
And every dead soul passes across these bridges.

The countless gigantic bridges intersect, intertwine, and spiral.

There is a twist of space-time here, and it is overcrowded with various souls.

It is like a scramble crossing of souls.

Every soul of every living thing from every era crosses this intersection.

At the middle of this crossing the soul of the man who lived the Heian Era,
and the soul of the boy who lived the Shadow of Tokyo happen to pass each other.
That instant, as if drawn to each other, the two souls intertwine.

Just like courting swallowtail butterflies.

The two souls dance in the air, and engage.

正しき愛よ

おまえは時を超えて

あらゆる壁を超えて

サピエンスの彼の岸へと　ぼくを連れていき

最後に見せたのは　真っ赤な砂浜

波音に聞こえるのは　Love me do... Love me do...

わかりきってたことだけど　僕は君を愛してる

Dear true love

You are timeless

Beyond every wall

To the Sapiens' other shore　You take me

And the last view you showed me　Was a scarlet seashore

What sounded like the waves were　Love me do… Love me do…

Although I already knew it　I love you

正しき愛よ

余は汝の似姿に幻滅し

余は汝の面影を溺愛し

母なる水面に　悠久の都の夢を見た

天翔る弓馬の先には　真っ赤な夕暮れ

浦波に聞こえしは　You know I love you...
You know I love you...

嗚呼　我は讃え　願い奉る　我が愛の永遠なれ

Dear true love

Thy image disenamored me

Thy shadows infatuated me

And on mother water's face　We have dreamt of an immortal city

Ahead of the winged martial horse　Was a scarlet sunset

And the waves sounded …　You know I love you …
You know I love you …

Oh I praise thee And humbly pray That my love be eternal

少年は、問いかけた。
「あなたは何をしてきたのですか?」
男は答えた。
「私は、荒ぶるものだ。」
男の背中には羽が生えていた。しかし少年は、それにはなんの疑念も持たなかった。
そして、男の目の中に映る、やはり羽が生えている自分自身を見つめて言った。
「僕は、泣いていました。オモカゲの中でただただ泣いていました。」
男の羽は風に乗って舞う。ひらひらと。
「その面影は私が作ったのだ。荒ぶりながら、全てをオモカゲにしてしまったのだ。」

少年は海を思い浮かべた。しかし、もう白黒ではなかった。
真っ赤に輝く茜色の太陽が、海には見えていた。
そして、真っ赤な海から聞こえる波の音色に、聞き惚れた。

「新しい世界の、はじまりを、夢見ていたのだ…」と男が口にしようとしたが、
その言葉は宙に舞い、少年には届かなかった。
少年はゆっくりと
「海に色をつけてくれてありがとうございました。」
とお礼を言った。

男の姿はもはやアゲハチョウそのものだった。

少年は、オモカゲの世界にはない声色で聞いた。

「そこに、愛はありましたか?」

アゲハチョウは天高く舞い上がり、遠い宙へと消えていた。

いつの間にか、少年の羽は消えていた。
少年はぐんぐんと落ちていた。風よりも早く、雷よりも激しく。
落ちながら、少年は、下界の世界を見渡した。
見渡して、驚いた。

世界に、色があったのだ。

地平線まで、どこまでも。見渡す限り、ありとあらゆるものに色があったのだ。

少年の脳裏に「カグノミヤ」という音が舞い降りた。

歓喜のあまり、彼は、色とりどりの声で叫んだ!

「僕は、落ちていくんだ! まだ見ぬ新しい世界、色のある世界、カグノミヤに!」

The boy asked,
"What did you do while you were alive?"
The man answered,
"I am the wild one."
There were wings on the man's back.
But the boy did not question the wings.
He just stared straight into the man's eyes
—where he could see a reflection of himself with wings—and said,
"I had been crying. I had just kept crying and crying in the Shadows."
The man's feathers danced in the wind. Softly.
"I created those shadows.
I went wild and turned everything into Shadows."

The boy recalled the sea. But it wasn't monochrome anymore.
He could see a madder red sun with scarlet rays, shining across the sea.
And he listened in fascination to the sound of
the waves coming from the scarlet sea.

"I had been dreaming of ... beginning ... a new world," the man tried to say,
But his words flew up into the air and didn't reach the boy.
The boy politely said,
"Thank you for coloring the sea,"
And expressed his gratitude.

The man had now completely taken the shape of a swallowtail butterfly.

The boy asked in a voice that did not exist in the world of Shadows.

Was there love there?

The swallowtail was there no more.
It had soared high into the sky and disappeared into thin air.

The boy's wings had disappeared without notice
The boy was falling with speed. Faster than the wind, and wilder than lightning.
As he fell, the boy looked around the world below him.
When he looked around, he was surprised.

The world had colors.

All the way to the horizon.
Everything had colors, as far as he could see to the horizon.

A music, or sound, "KAGUNOMIYA", echoed in his mind.

Out of pure joy, he shouted out in colorful voices!

**I'm going to fall all the way! All the way to the new world,
a world with colors, KAGUNOMIYA!**

少年が降り立った地球にも　まだヒトはいた。

地球は　もはや何もない空間では　なかった…。

そこは誰もがよく知る地球だった。

大地にはビルがそびえ立ち、銀色の光の筋が明るく伸びていた。
そうかと思うと、少年の手を引く透明な風が、
うすべに色の梅の花に挨拶し、青々とした大空へと舞い上がった。

モノクロだったトウキョウの街並みには、
レインボーカラーのアルファベットが踊り、
パステルカラーの自動車が、ひっきりなしに行き交っていた。

「この色であふれた世界を、香久之宮と名付けよう。」

少年は、色とりどりの世界を見て、そうつぶやいた。
ゆっくりと歩き出す少年の未来には、もうオモカゲはなく、
眩いばかりの光が差し込んでいた。
私たちの目の前を通って… 少年よ、どこへいくのだろうか？

＊

ああ、現在よ、未来へとつながる甘美な扉よ、
お前には色があったのだ。追いかけてくる過去を振り払うように、
現在は、新たな未来へと飛翔する。
さながら、羽化するアゲハチョウのように。

少年は、あらゆる色をみるだろう。
喪失と怯え、裏切りと嫉妬、孤独と不安、悲しみと虚無、
あらゆる色が待ち構えている。
それでも、色を見失うことは、少年にはもはや不可能だ。

そして、少年は問い続けるだろう。

ああ、愛よ、おまえの色をなんと名付けようか…！

Humans still lived in the earth that the boy landed in.

The earth was no longer an empty space ….

It was the Earth that we are all familiar with.

Buildings scraped the sky, stretching their silver lights.
Then one moment, the transparent wind leading the boy by his hand
greets the pink plum flowers and soars high up into the air.

The once monochrome city of Tokyo now has rainbow-colored alphabets
dancing all over it, and pastel-colored cars continually passing by.

"I shall name this world flooded with colors KAGUNOMIYA."

The boy said to himself, glancing at this colorful world.
There were no more Shadows in the boy's future,
but instead, it was lit by a glimmering bright light.
Passing right before us … boy, where are you headed to?

Oh, present time, thy sweet future's door, thou once hadst colors. As if to
push away the past whom always trails it from behind, the present soars
into a new future. Just like a swallowtail butterfly going through eclosion.

The boy shall see a countless variety of colors. Loss and fear, betrayal and
jealousy, loneliness and anxiety, sorrow and emptiness …
various colors are awaiting him. And still,
it is impossible for the boy to lose sight of the colors.

And the boy will keep asking.

Oh, love, what should I name your color … !

企画原案／玉塚 充 （タマプロ主宰 プロデューサー／ディレクター）
Producer / Director Mitsuru Tamatsuka

東京生まれ。舞台プロデューサーとして、明治座や東京芸術劇場などで様々な舞台の企画制作を手がける。代表作に「明治おんな橋」（山本富士子・主演）、「伝統芸能の若き獅子たち」（企画協力／世界文化社）等。ニューヨークでは５つの国際映画祭で上映された短編映画「firewater」の演出や、ベッシー賞受賞ダンサー作品「A Page Out of Order: M」の花道ムーブメントコーチを勤め、国際的なコラボレーションを展開。2016年にタマプロを立ち上げ、舞台作品のみならず、ライブアートから文化イベントまで、様々なクリエーターたちとコラボレートし、ジャンルの垣根をこえてアートワークを発信している。
【タマプロ関連アートプロジェクト】
Tama Pro: http://tama-pro.tumblr.com/
Sagi Tama: http://sagi-tama.sagiyama.com/

Born in Tokyo. As a theatre producer, he has produced various theatre productions at Meijiza Theater and Tokyo Metropolitan Theatre, including "Meiji Onna Bashi" (Starring Fujiko Yamamoto) and "The Young Lions of the Traditional Arts" (Co-produced by Sekaibunka Publishing Inc.). His credits in international collaborations include Executive Director for a short film "firewater" which was screened in five international film festivals in the US, and hanamichi movement coach for Bessie Awards dancer performance "A Page Out of Order: M". He founded Tama Pro in 2016, and ever since has collaborated with various creators from theatre to live arts and cultural events, and continues to deliver artworks that transcend artistic genres.
[Tama Pro related art projects]
Tama Pro: http://tama-pro.tumblr.com/
Sagi Tama: http://sagi-tama.sagiyama.com/

墨絵／渡邊ちょんと
Sumi-e Ink Art Chonto Watanabe

水墨画で伝統と現代的感性からダイナミックかつ繊細な独自の世界を創造し続ける画家・イラストレーター。新聞小説挿絵（伊東潤「茶聖」幻冬舎、相葉英雄「御用船帰還せず」幻冬舎、木下昌輝「決戦！新選組」日刊ゲンダイ 他）、建築物内装画（2020竹田市歴史文化交流センター）、書籍装丁画、TV番組用挿絵、広告、雑誌、舞台美術等、幅広く活動中。また、水墨画パフォーマンスではフェニックス 2019（カザン）、HINODE POWER JAPAN 2018（モスクワ）、日本大創立125周年慶祝典、XFLAG PARK幕張メッセ、他出演多数。岩手大学大学院農学研究科獣医学専攻修了。順天堂大学医学部衛生学教室助手を経て画業に専念。2019年大和市文化芸術賞受賞。神奈川県出身。
http://chonto.com/

Painter/illustrator. Merging tradition with a contemporary mind and using sumi-e (Japanese ink wash painting) technique, she creates a unique world that is both dynamic and delicate. Her wide range of works include illustrations for novel series in newspapers (Jun Ito, *Chasei*, Gentosha; Hideo Aiba, *Goyosen Kikan Sezu*, Gentosha; Masaki Kinoshita, *Kessen! Shinsengumi*, Nikkan Gendai, etc.), paintings within buildings (Takeda City Museum of Cultural History, 2020), book cover designs, illustrations for TV programs, advertisements, magazines, and scenography for theatres. Also, she has performed her sumi-e live performance in FENIX 2019 (Kazan), HINODE POWER JAPAN 2018 (Moscow), the 125th Anniversary Event for Nippon Sports Science University, XFLAG PARK Makuhari Messe, and many other events. She is a graduate of Iwate University, Graduate School of Agriculture, with a major in veterinary medicine. After working as an assistant professor for Juntendo University Department of Epidemiology and Environmental Health, she concentrated her career on painting. She was awarded the Cultural Arts Award from Yamato City in 2019. Her home town is Kanagawa.

物語／木村龍之介
Author of Story Ryunosuke Kimura

1983年大分県生まれ。東京大学文学部卒。演出家、作家。在学中より蜷川幸雄に演出を学び、2012年に劇団カクシンハンを設立。同年、シェイクスピア「ハムレット」を題材とした戯曲「ハムレット×SHIBUYA」を執筆し、演出。以降、「ハムレット」「夏の夜の夢」「マクベス」など、8年間で30作以上のシェイクスピア劇を演出する。俳優の起用は累計300名以上に登り、独自の演出メソッドを確立。現代と古典のクラッシュ（衝突）によって古典作品が持つ普遍性に新たな角度から光を当て、同時代のエンターテイメントとしてシェイクスピアをアップデートしている。創作活動と並行して、演技塾カクシンハン・スタジオを主宰し俳優の育成事業を行う傍ら、広くシェイクスピアや演劇の魅力を紹介するワークショップ講師として活動。文化事業での主な活動に「ほぼ日の学校」講師、早稲田大学や東京大学での講演会や、「三田文學」への寄稿など。戯曲作品「ハムレット×SHIBUYA」はイギリスの出版社Arden Shakespeareより翻訳出版されている。

Theatre director and writer. Born 1983 in Oita. Graduate of the University of Tokyo, Department of Literature. He studied direction under Yukio Ninagawa while he was still a student, and established Theatre Company KAKUSHINHAN in 2012. The same year, he wrote and directed his original script, "Hamlet x SHIBUYA", which was inspired by Shakespeare's *Hamlet*. Since then he has directed over 30 productions of Shakespeare plays in 8 years, including "Hamlet", "A Midsummer Night's Dream", and "Macbeth". He has worked with over 300 actors, and has devised his original directing method. By clashing tradition with contemporary, he illuminates the universality of the classical pieces, and updates Shakespeare plays as a contemporary entertainment. Aside from these creations, he runs an actors' training program KAKUSHINHAN STUDIO to guide aspiring actors, and lectures in various open workshops to introduce the fascination of theatre and Shakespeare. His other works in the cultural divisions include lectures in "Hobonichi School", symposiums at universities including the University of Tokyo and Waseda University, and essays for "Mita Bungaku". His script "Hamlet x SHIBUYA" was translated into English and published from Arden Shakespeare of UK.

英訳／岩崎 MARK 雄大
English Translation Yudai Mark Iwasaki

アメリカ出身。東京大学文学部英文科卒。幼少期をカナダ、アメリカで過ごし、英語ネイティブの日英バイリンガルとして語学の素養を習得する。俳優として、2014年より劇団カクシンハンの俳優としてシェイクスピア劇に連続出演する他、PARCO、東京芸術劇場などでの、海外アーティストとの公演・ワークショップに参画。同時に東京大学で学んだ語学の専門性と運用能力を多方面に活かし、論文、小説、エッセイ本、戯曲、ハリウッド映画脚本、大手広告会社の関連資料などの翻訳で活躍する。また、海外アーティストとの公演・ワークショップの通訳のほか、英語運用能力開発の専門家として、受験対策からビジネス英語まで幅広く英語の指導を行なっている。

Raised in USA. Graduate of the University of Tokyo, Department of English Literature. He spent his childhood years in Canada and the United States, where he developed native English proficiency and became an English/Japanese bilingual. He performed as an actor for Shakespeare plays in Theatre Company KAKUSHINHAN since 2014, and also participated in collaborative productions/workshops with international artists by PARCO Inc., and Tokyo Metropolitan Theatre. Alongside his career as an actor, he has utilized his English expertise and proficiency to translate various documents/literary pieces including theses, novels, essays, plays, Hollywood movie scrips, and papers for major advertising companies. He has also interpreted for international artists visiting Japan. He is also known for his expertise as an English educator, and he teaches English to a wide range of people for various purposes, ranging from entrance exams to business occasions.